P9-EAJ-640

Beyond Me

Also by
Annie Donwerth-Chikamatsu

Somewhere Among

Annie Donwerth-Chikamatsu

Beyond Me

A Caitlyn Dlouhy Book

ATHENEUM BOOKS FOR YOUNG READERS

New York London Toronto Sydney New Delhi

ATHENEUM BOOKS FOR YOUNG READERS
An imprint of Simon & Schuster Children's Publishing Division
1230 Avenue of the Americas, New York, New York 10020

Book design by Greg Stadnyk
Interior design by Irene Metaxatos
The text for this book was set in Guardi LT Std.
Manufactured in the United States of America
0420 FFG
First Edition
10 9 8 7 6 5 4 3 2 1
Library of Congress Cataloging-in-Publication Data
Names: Donwerth-Chikamatsu, Annie, author.
Title: Beyond me / Annie Donwerth-Chikamatsu.
Description: First edition. | New York : Atheneum Books for Young Readers, 2020. | "A Caitlyn Dlouhy Book." | Audience: Ages 8–12. | Audience: Grades 4–6. | Summary: In the aftermath of a major earthquake, eleven-year-old Maya overcomes her own fear to help others at home and in northeast Japan, where a tsunami caused great damage. Includes author's note about the facts behind the story.
Identifiers: LCCN 2019034919 (print) | LCCN 2019034920 (eBook) | ISBN 9781481437899 (hardcover) | ISBN 9781481437912 (eBook)
Subjects: CYAC: Novels in verse. | Earthquakes—Fiction. | Survival—Fiction. | Family life—Japan—Fiction. | Japan—Fiction.
Classification: LCC PZ7.5.D66 Bey 2020 (print) | LCC PZ7.5.D66 (eBook) |DDC [Fic]—dc23
LC record available at https://lccn.loc.gov/2019034919
LC eBook record available at https://lccn.loc.gov/2019034920

To the people of Japan,

especially

the people who work tirelessly

to keep us safe, warm, and fed

MARCH 9, 2011

not much time
between good morning and good-bye

out the door

early

Father goes one way
to catch a train east to Shinjuku

then later

I go another way
to walk to school

when all's clear

Mother goes to the table
to work at her laptop

out into March wind
I rush to meet Yuka
my best friend since kindergarten

Maya! she shouts to me

we run, grab hands
    lean in, squint, and
    smile into each other's faces

we are sweaterless

kaze no ko
"wind kids"
who don't wear coats
even in winter

with no time to spare

to be on time

we hurry on

at recess

a time

when we choose
how we use

our time,

Yuka and I run out

to meet
under the cherry tree near the gym

long time no see, I say

she giggles

Ready?

Yuka stands behind me

waiting
waiting
waiting
for
the wind to knock me back

into her outstretched arms

it takes big gusts and trust
to fall back

it's not easy

for me to let go

there's hesitation

then panic
the moment my toes are off the ground

then relief—

Yuka's always there

to catch me

today's wind is not a true March wind
but
we wait
    let go and
    fall
as many times as we can
until the playground clock says

our time is up

back inside
my class lines up

carrying our chairs
to the music room
we're out of step
starting and stopping
bumping and scooting
straggling

before lunch each day
these last days of fifth grade
we practice
for the spring choir performance
at the city concert hall
on Monday
March 14

five days from now

parents (mostly mothers) and grandparents
will come

at their appointed time

make their way through the lobby then

rush to seats
as each grade files onstage
                    takes their places
                    sings and exits

Teacher chose me
to be front row center
to clank blocks
to keep the beat
with her piano chords

I love this task
but
it's not easy

each day
we get lost

in bird notes

a thrush
high in mulberry branches
outside the music room

begins his song when we begin ours

he is trying to cheer us up—
our song sounds so sad

humans are fragile, we sing

Teacher assures us
the song will make hearts ring

it does end on a higher note

but it is no one's favorite

except
maybe grandparents'

we struggle on

with my *clank clank*

trying to get them in tune

life is mysterious, we sing

walls
windows
tree limbs shudder

the thrush disappears in flutters

Teacher stands up

11:45 *earthquake*

we don't miss a beat
grabbing our padded emergency hoods
from the backs of our chairs
putting them
on our heads
in case something falls

we have earthquakes all the time
but this time
Earth rocks us
in circles

someone says, *this is eerie*

Earth stills

we settle back into our classroom

where

there are desks to slide under
if it happens again

it doesn't

early afternoon
in the gym

all fifth-grade classes
come together
to practice
Moriyama's big hit, "Sakura"
a spring song for cherry blossom season
we will perform at the sixth graders'
  graduation ceremony

after they present us with rice seeds from their
  school project

they will stand from their chairs
to face us

as we sing

I know we will see them smile

we are in harmony
from the first note

the thrush does not take a seat
in the cherry tree outside the gym

shoulder to shoulder

within the group

I lift my eyes to the windows

singing the chorus

Sakura! Sakura!
as these cherry blossoms bloom . . .

I see
sparrows flit and twitter
twig to twig
through cherry blossom buds
not ready to bloom

after school
I wait for Yuka

not in a rush
on Wednesdays
we walk and chat
pass shops and stop
to count

pigeons sitting
in a bare tree,

bulbuls shredding
magnolias, and

city workers pruning
branches

the trees are full today, I say

Yuka giggles
I giggle back

we count
twelve pigeons
three bulbuls
five city workers

then cut along the path
of Great-grandfather's field
past the last cabbage
daikon and
broccoli

he's pushing a motor tiller
guiding it
making a new row of crops

a starling follows him
picking out insects

I call to him
Yuka echoes me
then says,
he cannot hear us

he doesn't hear well anyway
and
he never says much either

even back when
I followed behind him

helping him
picking out weeds
and
planting bowls of seeds
            buckets of taro tubers, and
            trays of edamame seedlings

before I got too busy

with school
      cram school and
      English practice

Great-grandfather has farmed full-time since
  age seventeen
for sixty-three years

each year I think will be his last

his customers pass his vegetable stand
with bicycle baskets packed
with vegetables, toilet paper, and detergent

“one-stop shopping” at the new store
kills his business
but still
he tills, sows, and gathers

each season

there is always something
to do

he plants less, but
we always have plenty to eat

Grandmother pickles the excess

the starling pecks the softened soil

a wagtail zigs and zags and wags

Great-grandfather's fields feed them, too

Yuka asks, *same birds from yesterday?*

I don't know

same from last year?

I don't know how long they live

I only know their names and
          their songs
mainly
I just love them

how they appear out of nowhere
like an unexpected gift

how they come and go
     fly in and out
          as they please
          as they need

over a garden wall
we hear but do not see
a bush warbler

at the park
two doves
blink at us from their fence seat

and greet us with *coo*

we stop to inspect the cherry tree

one branch hangs down and reaches out to us

the blossom-viewing prediction for Tokyo is right,
  we agree,
no way
this tree will bloom before a new school year
  begins April 6
no way
we will picnic under full blossoms the last days
  of our break, but
no matter

tight buds
Yuka and I

enjoy now together

we take our time
before
we have to start our evening schedules

today
for her, abacus lessons
for me, English practice

see you!

we say to the doves
and to each other

and turn

Yuka
left

I
right

Grandmother is bringing in laundry
at the house Great-grandfather built

I stop at our gates sitting side by side

the daffodils Mother planted
the fall Grandfather died

wait to open

a breeze through their house
reaches me

paper, straw, wood
cold and dark
the house smells sunny
like vegetables
freshly cut or drying

Grandmother always takes a break
from the vegetable stand
to bring in their laundry
to greet me when I return and
to help me while Mother works

at our house
doors slam

the wind, says Grandmother and smiles

I yell, *I'm home,* toward our open living-dining room
window

Mother yells back,

Maya, you're late!

she sets aside time
on Wednesdays, my break from cram school,
to give me English lessons in listening
reading
writing
and computer skills in both languages

she was born in America
grew up an orphan in foster homes
came here
married Father, the language, and the culture
and opened a translating service

I have two languages
two cultures
two passports

I have roots and wings
(Mother tells me often)
but
I have only been to America once

still
I know it pretty well
    its food
    its music
    its history

Mother chooses my favorite subjects to research, too

today
she has prepared a research and
        note-taking exercise from a video
about
the smallest, most delicate bird in the world

it can fly through bad weather
    balance midair
    and
    hover
    paddling its wings in infinity symbols

it can sip from breeze-blown flowers
    darting to adjust to their sudden movements

it is strong and cute and beautiful
at the same time

its feathers sparkle and
        change with the angle of sunlight
like a rainbow

its name is "Humming Bird"
(Mother corrects my spelling)

sadly
this bird, this jewel, stays only in the Americas

MARCH 10, 2011

near the end of the school year

it's not easy to stay
on the same page
in class
and
on the same note
in choir practice
and
on the chair
in cram school

after trying to stay awake in cram school
I rush to do homework

I sip tea
from my favorite mug
  the mug Yuka gave me in second grade

        when
        we had time for fun
        before
        we started cramming for
        junior high entrance exams

MARCH 11, 2011

in the morning rush

07:44 Earth shudders
enough

to make us pause
note the time and
watch the pendant light stir the air
above the dining table

my cell phone dings from its drawer

Yuka texts

I text 

I put my phone back in its place
and run to meet her

it's a perfect spring day

who wants to be inside?

at morning practice
the thrush is not outside the music room

we are all on the same note

but our hearts are still not in the song

at recess
no wind to push us down
Yuka and I join others
for a game of circle catch

at afternoon practice
in the gym
we are caught up in song

we are ninety fifth graders in tune

our voices flow
            blend
            soar

Sakura! Sa———ku—

a bell rings

lights flicker

the gym clock says

2:46

the floor jiggles ///////////////\\\|||||\\\\////////
|||\\\\///\\\\//////////>>>>>>>>>//////////<<<<<\\\\\\\\<<<<<<||||
this will be over >>>>>>/\/\/\/\\\\<>>>|||<<<<<>>>/\/\||||/\\

\||||||||||>||<||>||<||>||<||>||<||<>|||| ||||| <>>>>>>>><><||||||||||
><><><>||||||||||<>/\/\\/\\\/\/\<<<<|////////// any <><><><
>>>><><>///<>>>\\\\\\ second

////||||||||<><><><<<<<<<<>
|——————————|||——————————————

to the walls!

Earth

d
r
o
p
s

below me

midair

toes off the floor

hovering

arms paddling

free-falling

feels like an eternity

before

I drop

backward

Yuka?

is she okay?

standing

falling

to

my

knees

crawling

we're scrambling

to the walls

shoulders to shoulders

backs to the wall

ceiling squares dangle

CRASH

the basketball net lets go of the ceiling

and swings down into play

Out!

outside

we gather by Teacher

the playground clock

dodges tree branches

the school building

bucks //pitches\\ groans

room by room

windows slide one way

then back

desks rattle-// scrape the floor

kids yelp

the intercom garbles Principal's words

we huddle with Teacher's words

calming us

Earth stills

the playground clock tells us
five minutes have passed

we fifth graders are sitting on the playground
caught without our emergency hoods
wearing our indoor shoes

no one mentions it

14:54 we are still
14:55
14:57
14:58 whirling
15:01 everyone is calm
15:02 cooperative and
15:03 mostly
15:05 quiet
15:06 even when Earth
15:07
15:08 jolts us
15:08
15:11 we are following the rules
15:12
15:13

other students file out of the main building
wearing their emergency hoods
scooting into their outdoor shoes

15:15 everyone drops to the ground

at the school gate
Yuka's mother, other mothers
are suddenly there
waiting for the signal to enter
like they're supposed to

fifth-grade teachers stand
do head counts then
call roll

some mothers squat close to the ground
to avoid
15:18 falling down
others
15:19 squeal and fall
most try to stand ready

all of them look
15:20 worried

15:21

15:23 stunned

15:25 scared

school staff bring our outdoor shoes
from the entrance
telling us we will not go back inside

we put them on

using a foghorn
Principal tells us the epicenter was up north
praises us for cooperating obediently
moving quickly
sitting quietly

says we can check out with teachers
if a family member is here

tells us to be careful
watchful
helpful
wishes us well

Yuka's mother leads her away

we wave

Grandmother is in line
my first word to her
after Teacher signs me out is

Mother?

she's watching the house

we take a back way
away from the shopping area
like Grandmother tells me to do
in emergencies

to avoid falling plaster, signs, glass

we stay in the middle of the street
no cars, no bicycles, no people
around

it's quiet

except
for a rumble starting
moving along the street
15:28 pushing streetlights
trees
houses
garden gates
walls

electrical lines bounce
high to low

we drop down
with
no cover
Grandmother shields me

I hold on to her

15:29 my head spins
15:30 stomach churns
15:31 is Earth still spinning?
15:33 we wait until the lines barely swing

we walk on
arm in arm
stop
15:34 drop

15:35
15:36 the wires keep moving
15:37 up
15:37 down

I cannot feel the ground beneath my feet
so
I let her guide me
knowing she is mindful of all above us
below us and
around us
she keeps our distance from garden walls

15:38 we drop
wait
walk
15:41 drop
wait
walk
15:42 drop
15:42 wait
walk

15:44 a brick crashes near us
like the wall threw it

15:48 everything feels like it's spinning

15:49
15:52 it's all a blur
15:54
15:54
15:55

until

we make it to the fields

15:57 we drop

Great-grandfather is sitting behind the tiller

he waves to us
he's okay
we're okay

we move on

near the park

15:59 tree limbs and
electrical wires flap
we wait

to head toward our gates

16:00 I feel I am floating
16:01
16:03 my feet never
16:03 touch
16:03
16:04 the
16:04 ground

until

we reach our porch

we step over something
dark, crumbled

the swallows' nest

smashed when it crashed
from the eaves

Grandmother says, *take care*
hugs me and
heads next door

I drop my school indoor shoes
push out of outdoor shoes
into slippers (in case of broken glass)
run to the living-dining room

16:09 the pendant light is circling the table

everything is in place
except
Mother is under the table
    typing
    e-mailing
    texting
    Skyping
    helping foreign clients

she looks up
    shouts,
    come!

16:10 I drop down
  take cover beside her and
  hold on to her

she hugs me
    and
    says,

glad you're home

there's no cell phone call service

Father hasn't answered her texts or e-mails
but she knows
he's okay

he always forgets to charge his battery

his building is new
            earthquake proof
            far from the bay

we're not getting the worst of it

she switches on the TV

the TV is stable
anchored to the wall

at the top of the screen
a map of Japan flashes
tsunami warnings

for

all

eastern coasts

we are secure under the table

miles from the epicenter
miles from Tokyo Bay

we are safe from the ocean

newscasters are reporting updates
16:12 their floor groans
their desk rocks
16:12 their chairs tumble
16:12 they struggle to sit up

the camera cuts to a map
showing the epicenter of the quake
northeast
far from us

then cuts to footage of
water spilling over a seawall up north
news offices shaking
a fire raging at an oil refinery near Tokyo

they tell us to take care about aftershocks
and home fires

16:13 everything rattles there
16:13 our TV jerks

the camera goes back to newscasters

they are wearing helmets!

16:14 they are shaken but try to remain calm
16:16
16:17

16:20 Earth *pushes*

16:25 rolls

16:28 punches hard

with each move
I see
hear and
feel
every board in this house
flex and
bend

braces, adhesives, and cabinet doors
keep our things
in place
but

16:30 the house
16:31 never
16:31
16:32 seems
16:33 to
16:35 stop
16:38 spinning

the landline telephone rings
Father is okay
he says
they're checking the building
so
he's not at his computer

his cell phone battery is dead
so
he can't text
so
he had to stand in line to use a pay phone

he asks about everyone and
                    house damage
Mother says everyone
                    everything is okay
                    electricity
                    water pipes
                    gas lines

when I tell him the only thing knocked down is the
  swallows' nest
he says, *they will rebuild it*

but this house shakes a lot like it's going to fall

he tells me wooden houses are built to move
our house is new and
built well but
tells me to stay under the table or

to go to the fields if I'm worried
and
reminds me what we all know:

to be mindful of falling roof tiles
garden walls
electrical lines, etc.

all trains have stopped and
bus lines are unsure

rails and roads need to be inspected for damage

because Earth is moving

he will walk home

and call on the way
if he finds a pay phone

be careful,
we tell each other

Mother runs out to the fields
mindful of everything
to tell Grandmother
Father is okay

I sit at the table
Earth is not moving
or is it?

16:42 the pendant light swirls

16:43

16:44 then jerks
my phone dings from its drawer
Mother tells me to get the charger too
to keep it charged
to be ready
in case we lose electricity

Yuka texts

no cram school today

my response
describes how I feel

freaked out
dizzy

16:45 swirling is not any

16:47 better than

16:49 shakes

16:49

17:00
17:01
17:03
17:04
17:07
17:10
17:12 we are safe
17:15
17:15
17:16
17:19 under the table
17:27
17:27
17:28
17:31
17:32
17:35
17:35
17:38
17:40
17:40 no crashing
17:43
17:54
17:58
18:04
18:06
18:19
18:20

18:37

18:38

18:55

18:57

19:10

19:15

19:19

19:20 smashing or

19:35 leaking

19:36

19:45

19:46

20:00

20:03

20:07

20:10

20:13

20:16

20:20 is
20:36
20:41
20:44
20:46 THIS
20:56
21:00
21:13
21:15
21:24
21:35
21:49 really
21:56
21:59
22:00
22:03
22:14
22:15
22:16
22:34
22:47
22:56
23:00 real?
23:31
23:44
23:53
23:56 I splinter into a heap
23:57
23:58

DAY 2

00:06
00:07
00:13 am I awake?
00:15
00:19 is the ground moving?
00:22
00:24
00:32
00:42 yes
00:53
02:05
02:08
02:17
02:23
02:30
03:11 again
03:17

03:44 and again
03:45
03:59 and again

did I sleep through some?

04:02

04:02

04:08

04:24 am I dreaming?

04:26

04:31

04:31

04:45

04:46

04:58

05:11

05:23

05:25

05:34 I want to be dreaming

06:34

06:48

under the table
I wake exhausted

Mother is beside me at work
typing
e-mailing
comforting
advising
helping
her foreign clients on
her laptop plugged into the extension cord

next to her
sits
the landline telephone and
next to me
sits
an empty noodle cup

I don't remember eating

I remember Grandmother checking on us
                                                        bringing pickles
                                                        filling the hot-water pot
I don't remember hearing the telephone ring or
                                                        Mother talking to Father

a shopkeeper let him use his telephone
she says

he left the office later than he wanted
and
    started home later than he wanted

he's okay

and still on his way

Earth does not move
through breakfast
I put away our cereal bowls and
  sit to finish my tea

my mug wobbles
          sloshes
07:36 falls over

I grab it
  dart under the table

tea runs
   spills
   drips over the edge

I stay under the table
clutching my mug

08:59 *ding*

a text from Yuka

09:00 *all is still shaky but okay*

(some broken dishes)

at her house

Yuka can't text much

she has to pay attention

to stay on her toes

to be ready

me too, I text

she sends ☺

I text *later*

no emoji shows my feeling

09:01 I don't

09:02 feel

09:03 like

09:05 smiling

until

our front gate

opens and closes

Father!

we greet him in the doorway with hugs and kisses and tears

we are shocked to see him
in green glow-in-the-dark sports shoes
with his polished businessman shoes
tied by their laces
dangling around his neck

he bought the only comfortable shoes
left on the shelf
to walk the twenty kilometers home

on his way
shops handed out
                    food and water
to everyone walking home

he helped put out a pan fire
at a ramen shop kitchen

along the way

he saw

a fallen shop sign

a leaning tree

a broken electrical wire

Father hands me a paper bag

he bought *sakura mochi*
from a shopkeeper who served him tea

one for me and one for Mother
(Great-grandfather and Grandmother don't eat
sweets)

the house
09:45 jerks

10:00 rattles
with each jolt
Father shouts
jumps under the table and
says,
wooden houses shake . . .

a lot!
I say,
our house must be near a fault line

he says,
all Japan is near a fault line

my face shows him
that was the wrong thing to say

10:04 after more clattering

10:12 shaking

he crawls out

    checks gas lines

            water pipes and

            electrical wires

    comes back

    looks relieved

he goes out to the fields

    checks on Great-grandfather and Grandmother

    asks them to stay at our house tonight

he's thinking

newer

stronger

they're thinking

older

more trusted

10:24

10:25

Father turns on the TV

he and I stand together
watching
horrified
seeing

scenes of yesterday's tsunami
along the northeastern coast

for the first time

we see how bad it is

I cannot bear to watch but I cannot turn away

where are the people?

I lose my breath
catch my breath
hold my breath

I search each frame
but
I don't see anyone

only the ocean

the ocean flowing
over seawalls

the ocean pushing cars, boats, vans
down streets
past shops
into shops

the ocean crushing
a stand of pine trees

the ocean rushing across fields
streets
houses

the ocean splashing
a swirling whirlpool

like it is going down a drain

I look at Father

it is the first time I've seen him cry

up there

at 2:46 p.m. Friday afternoon

were students practicing for their choir concert
  like us?

were kindergartners already home?

were first graders walking home?
were their mothers rushing to find them
                                        to rescue them
                                        to run to higher ground?

were farmers in fields like Great-grandfather
  and Grandmother?
were people in shops, offices, homes like Father
  and Mother?
were they worried about things falling on them
  as they ran?

          did everyone escape?

the TV only shows us the ocean moving beyond the shore

then

there are "day after" photos and coverage

people stranded
on school rooftops

people standing
in front of homes
offices
shops
ripped from their foundations

boats and cars
on top of or inside
buildings and houses barely standing

people separated from their family
from their friends
from their community

people looking for people

people alone

one pine
stands
alone

each tree beside it
washed away with the ocean

one lone pine is the only one left behind

it is a miracle

Mother doesn't watch the footage
saying
she doesn't need to see it
                                        to know it
                                        to feel it

she had read about it online

10:34 I dash under the table

and watch warnings flash
along the coasts on the map of Japan
above the sad coastal scenes

and hear details of
a damaged nuclear energy plant
close to the coast

the company struggles to keep it safe
their workers risk their lives

the government declares a state of emergency

10:43 aftershocks continue

10:46 here
10:47 and there

experts expect aftershocks and tsunami
the same scale or bigger

so

it may be worse

people of the Northeast!

aftershocks threaten
there
the ocean threatens
there
the nuclear energy plant threatens
there

many of you are without food, water, electricity,
shelter,

family

there
is so much worse than
here

here
the quake was so strong
it bent the antenna on Tokyo Tower

here
the aftershocks are not as strong as there

here
airports, subway and train lines are closed

Father will stay home

until Tokyo reopens

11:37

Mother checks her e-mail
            types frantically
            asks me to help Grandmother
at their house

the mess is more than I expected

nothing is broken

just out of place

thing after thing
we put up
            down but mostly
            away
behind cupboard doors
we secure with string

it's inconvenient but
they will not fly open again

we stand together
looking at the uncluttered room

something is missing

Grandfather's retirement clock still ticks

its hands move
but do not keep time

its pendulum swung in half turns
                                        half turn right
                                        half turn left
now it spins in circles

on unstable ground

the clock has lost its chime

and

11:47 I have lost my trust in Earth

tears fill my eyes
and then I feel guilty

TV images fill my head

people of the Northeast have lost

so much

❦ ❦ ❦

no pipes are broken
we can use tap water

11:59

12:01 standing on the quaking kitchen floor
it's too dangerous to boil, steam, or fry

we use the electric pot
for "just add water" meals

I am thankful for Grandmother's homemade pickled vegetables

12:11

12:28

12:34

12:54

13:04

13:37

13:43

13:47

Father makes tea to have with the *sakura mochi*

14:14 the tea quivers in my mug

in their cups

14:21

no one says anything

15:18

15:44 we are going through the motions

15:57 while Earth keeps moving

16:54

for dinner
we eat rice and steamed vegetables made in the rice
cooker

19:53 the house jumps

20:46 shakes
21:01 rattles

rests a while

21:53 then reminds us

22:14

22:15 strongly
to place our coats and shoes
next to our beds

I pull my chair away from my desk
so I can jump under

23:03

an emergency ladder rolled up in a tube
sits in a corner of my room
23:14 I hope I never need it

23:37

DAY 3

00:56

05:32

05:41

07:12 Earth quivers
I measure the strength by
07:13 the pendant light
07:13 swirls

07:44

08:24 this one is larger than a swirl
we turn on the TV
to check the magnitude
and see

a man was rescued
out in the sea
from his rooftop

his wife is missing
thousands are missing

the Japanese rescue team returned
from helping New Zealand
after their big earthquake

Japan's Self-Defense Forces work with the US military
for recovery and relief

many nations ask to help

over ten thousand people may have been killed
millions have no food and water

we eat our porridge and pickles in gratitude

we hear that
yesterday
while we were having tea and *mochi*
an explosion at the damaged nuclear
energy plant injured four workers
a radiation leak may get bigger
and
over 100,000 people were ordered to
evacuate
from the area

the prime minister says
this is Japan's most difficult crisis since the
bombings
in World War II

08:55 we swirl
and

08:57 keep swirling

our world is spinning
spiraling like it's
circling a drain

I hear Mother tell Father
she read that

a professor at Tokyo's Earthquake
Institute says

Tokyo
should prepare for a large quake

prepare

at home
we have emergency supplies
in storage

at school
every September 1
on the anniversary of the 1923 earthquake
that demolished Tokyo
we drill earthquake and fire preparedness

on March 11
our fifth-grade classes were caught in the gym

we weren't prepared
to calmly walk out
wearing emergency hoods and outdoor shoes

experts always mention "The Big One"
that will hit Tokyo again

is it coming soon?

a university professor says to prepare

the March 11 earthquake off the northeast shore
was so strong

it pushed Japan's main island eastward
created a massive tsunami and
slashed the eastern coastline in size

it shifted Earth's axis and
changed its rotation

it sped up time and
shortened the length of day
by
1.8 microseconds

Tokyo skyscrapers swayed
shops
schools
houses shook violently

small fires ignited

what would "The Big One" under Tokyo do?

prepare?

nothing can prepare you for bigger ones

09:32 than this

09:41

10:26 this

11:23 and this

how much more can this house stand?

can it stand "The Big One"?

with rapid thoughts
    rapid heartbeat
    rapid breath

I run out
    past shoes
    through door and gate
into open field

I want to fly
into open sky

out of breath

I fall to my knees
then back
onto open space

I lay my hands and bare feet on Earth
  dig in
  gulp, almost
  pass out

I catch my breath
in and out
I breathe
in and out
I release my fear
in and out

nothing can fall on me

here

Earth
sun
sky
wind
all

here

I am not alone

behind a plastic sheet covering a seed bed

a shadow
stops, settles, and huddles

farther afield

Great-grandfather runs a rope between stakes
                                    pulls it taut
                                    snaps it
to mark a row

11:32 he shifts from one foot to another
    inches along
    places a seed from a chipped rice bowl
one by one by one
into the soil
equal distance apart

11:48 he waits

turns, hands behind his back,
drags his foot alongside
covering the row with soil
seed by seed by seed

these steps he repeats
row by row by row

11:51 he loses his rhythm, his pace

but he keeps going

I cannot tell if the ground is moving

I breathe in

out
in
out

all is still
in and
out

I look over my shoulder toward the house

Father is checking the gas
                                the pipes
                                the foundation

still
the house stands

here
everything looks the same

here, there

everything is different

Father calls me in to lunch
I look back to the fields and

12:01 dig my hands and toes deeper into Earth

the shadow is gone

at the table
no one mentions the dirt beneath my fingernails

12:34 two shallow aftershocks
12:45 closer to us

ding
a message from Yuka
hang in there
with no emoji
I send her the same message

Mother is headlong into reaching out
organizing
gathering things
to help the people of the Northeast

Father asks me to go to the one-stop shop

people are out
like a normal day
except

a sign on the door requests limiting
bread and rice purchases
and
the "heart" and "love" signs
        chocolates
        and
        flowers for White Day
have been put away

tomorrow
no one will celebrate this day
the Valentine's Day
for only girls and women

no lights are on
the store is conserving electricity

fish
wrapped in plastic
shimmer
even without case lighting

poor fishermen!

for some of them

this may have been their last catch

❦ ❦ ❦

cashier lines wind through the store
customers buy just for the day
their handbaskets almost empty

I ask why
our basket has two bottles of water
prepackaged meals
tea

we have supplies at home

Father says, *to donate*

access to some areas is taking time
relief centers do not accept fresh vegetables and fruit
from the public now

13:12 *jostled*
my heart pounds

we're surrounded by shelves of packaged snacks
nothing moves
no one moves
no one loses their place in line

Father considers a chocolate bar
for you and Mother, he says

we decide not to buy it

when he hands Mother the shopping bag
he says, *not much*

she says, *this helps, thank you*

Father sleeps through
the afternoon
on the floor next to us at the table

14:59 I duck under the table

Mother hands me origami paper

a group in America, Students Rebuild,
asks people to make a crane
take a photo
post it on their page

with a message to the people of Japan

she shows me their Facebook and Twitter pages

children and adults have made cranes

the group's logo is a red dot like the Japanese flag
with a crane-shaped piece missing

the red crane is flying
out and away
from the red dot

I fold a red paper
  and
  press
  and
  open it

to release
a flying crane

this red crane carries

my message
within its folds

Dear People of the Northeast,

My heart is broken for you.

from Maya

Mother uploads the photo
onto the group's page
and her page
with the message
"Carry On"

she receives over fifty "likes"

the doorbell rings
a neighbor hands over
the neighborhood clipboard
telling us to read then pass along to
Grandmother, the next and last person on the list

the clipboard reminds us of emergency procedures
informs us of possible energy blackouts
starting tomorrow
and
schedules us for the fire alert group

Father returns from delivering the clipboard
reporting Great-grandfather and Grandmother are fine
after a hard day's work

they are eating dinner in a darkening room

❦ ❦ ❦

Mother has already restricted gas and electricity use and
has turned off the toilet seat heater

sitting by solar lamplight

I hear
in the distance
growing stronger
louder
closer

clank! clank!

our neighborhood group
walks along the streets
striking sticks
and chanting

Watch out for fire!

clank! clank!

in winter
neighbors follow a list
taking turns
making the rounds
warning us to be mindful of heaters

now

clank! clank!

they warn us to be mindful of emergency candles

fires are a big danger
anytime

now
everything is moving and
March winds are blowing

I worry about broken gas pipes
and
electrical wires
when the house shifts

20:37 especially when it's strong

and

29:56 shallow

wooden houses sitting close together
move
a lot

we are being

21:27 hit

21:44 from all directions

21:53 two at the same time

21:53

22:16 a closer

stronger one

I feel
myself shatter
into a thousand shards

bird shaped

flying out
in all directions

23:28 I shelter the red crane
in my hands
under my pillow

hoping

Earth will be still

this nightmare will end

and I will sleep

DAY 4

00:10

01:47

02:01
02:29
02:55

04:16
04:59

aftershocks are closer to us

earlier
people in the Northeast woke (if they slept)
to sirens and broadcast warnings

with
another tsunami alert
for the coast

it's a false alarm

with
a warning
to be careful of aftershocks

07:16

the announcement of
no choir concert today
passes through our class telephone tree

the city hall and school are under inspection

no school until further notice
we are asked to stay close to home

07:20

in the news

up there
officials in white protective gear
check children for radiation

down here
city offices post on the Internet
a list of blackouts and
a guide to appliance consumption

the government encourages offices and businesses
to close to save energy
all trains have stopped
except one section of one train line—
the Keio line from our station to Father's office stop

Father is going to work

he packs a shirt

                underwear and

                razor for the office

he may not make it back

I don't want him to go
I don't want to worry about him
but
I walk out with him and
  hug him good-bye
he stops to look out to the fields

Great-grandfather strides toward a patch
with his hoe resting on his shoulder

good, eh?
Father's voice cracks

he puts his salaryman bag on his shoulder
    rests a hand on mine
    tells me to take care

I tell him too

I watch him head to his job
at a computer
in a cubicle in Tokyo

Father trusts the structure of things

he works with numbers

and whatever he does
counts

I watch Great-grandfather

he strikes Earth with the hoe
turns the soil
loosens it
moves forward
strikes it again

08:41 he keeps going

working
here
now
by hand

the starling follows him
pecking the soil

it is the only bird around

no bulbuls scavenge old crops

no crows swoop the skies

no doves coo

no thrush trills

no birds sing

this is a silent spring
morning

08:53

Great-grandfather strikes Earth
turns the soil
loosens it
moves forward
strikes again
and again and
again
like Earth will still be beneath him
like there will still be a harvest
like there will still be a future

Mother waves at me
standing next to her bicycle

she is waving to get my attention
but I wave back like "good-bye"
knowing she wants me to join her
                                        to gather goods
                                        to drop off
at relief centers

she moves on without me

09:01

10:02

11:11

sitting at the table with Mother
her phone dings
it's an aftershock alert app

the phone
dingdingdingdingdingdingdings
before aftershocks
and
during
15:12 dingdingdingdingdingdingding
dingdingdingdingdingdingding

dingdingdingdingdingdingding
15:16 dingdingdingdingdingdingding
dingdingdingdingdingdingding

dingdingdingdingdingdingding
15:17 dingdingdingdingdingdingding
dingdingdingdingdingdingding

the frantic dinging lasts longer than the shock

I ask her to turn it off
she does

she goes back to pen to paper
there is no blackout
but
we could lose power

she's saving computer battery energy
scrawling notes
planning the next stage of her relief effort

she asks me to help
shop and drop donations
by bicycle

and
tells me
I can lighten the weight of caring by helping

but
15:52 with each movement
no matter how small

16:25 I lose my footing

18:07

the death toll grows
but no one knows
for sure
how many are lost

getting relief
to affected regions is still not easy

we need good news

like the baby found alive
under rubble
after she was swept
from her mother's arms
by the tsunami

she is reunited with her parents
who survived

this miracle, this joy
lightens

a little

but
the nuclear problem grows
19:25 more unstable
with each day

the company tells us it is working hard
but
Mother's clients tell her the news coverage is alarming
from outside Japan

their radiation fears grow
stronger
with each report

20:03 and for me
20:06 with each tremble

when Father comes home
I want to confide I cannot face
all this sadness and fear

instead of saying

I am worried about radiation
fires and
"The Big One"

I say,
it's not easy for me
to help Mother help others

he is slow to respond
then
asks me if I remember flying to America

remember what the flight attendant told us
to do
if air masks fall?

put yours on first
then help others

strengthen yourself, he tells me

I lie awake thinking

strengthen myself

how?

I am afraid
expecting
dreading the next tremor
but
I am off guard
reacting
fumbling my way
under the table

I go to the table
stand and
on a piece of origami paper
I write:

Dear People of the Northeast,

Each time Earth moves I am knocked off my feet.
I will find a way to strengthen myself.

from Maya

I fold
  press and
  release

with each gesture
I think of the people in the Northeast
and hope for everyone's safety

I fold
  press
  release

  fold
  press
  release

  slowly
  deliberately

with each gesture
I breathe
Earth, be calm

fold press fold press fold press

I cannot tell if Earth is listening

but with each gesture
I feel calmer

I bend the crane's bowing head
  pull its spreading wings
          releasing it and
  set it on the table

is that a spasm? a quiver? a tremble?

the ceiling is too dark to check the pendant light
but then
23:50 Earth **jolts** strong enough to know

I don't dart under the table
I hover
I want to fly away

the paper crane flits and flaps across the table

I grab on to its neck
we are off

through clouded skies
on paper wings
we fly
north
past Tokyo
past the nuclear energy plant
past the earthquake epicenter

to the one pine standing alone on the shore
after the tsunami ripped the others away

the crane's neck bows
I slide onto the branch beside it

I have never seen such darkness

no light anywhere

I cannot see what is lost beyond
but I feel it
all

cool unirradiated wind from the north washes over me

beneath me
I feel warmth, life
rising and descending
from and to the tree roots

splintered and scarred
still, this tree stands
alone

shaken and scarred
still, many people stand
alone

at the arc of one aftershock
23:51 Earth quakes again

one minute has passed between these two aftershocks

I am back

in bed

DAY 5

1:36

I sleep

03:41

04:59

deeply

06:09

until

the dingdingdingdingdingdingding of the alarm clock

or

07:04 Mother's phone app?

it's the alarm

they are up getting ready for the day

I go to the table

Dear People of the Northeast,

I am worried for you and for me. Making cranes makes me calm.

I will make 1,000! I will think good thoughts for us.

from Maya 💔

12:20

after lunch
I text Yuka to meet

her mother hesitates letting her come

out
under scattered clouds

we fall into each other's arms

it's colder than winter
we're both wearing coats
both sad and worried

she tells me she's staying inside
under the table
I tell her folding cranes makes me calm
so
I will fold one thousand

she wants to join me
comes home with me and
calls her mother

14:28 we
15:56 ride out
15:56 Earth's
16:03 movements

together

we will fold one thousand cranes

together

we fold and press

we bend their heads bowing
downward
  but
  keep their wings pointing
skyward

to string them
to send them to the people of the Northeast
to let them know we are thinking of them
      we are wishing them well and
      we are carrying on for them

but send to which area?

the destruction is massive

who will accept them?
a tsunami survivor shelter?
a radiation evacuee shelter?

accepting the cranes and
finding a place for them
may be a burden

we are all overwhelmed
all over Japan

Mother suggests sending them
to Students Rebuild in America

they will donate money
for each crane
to help all the people in the Northeast

Yuka and I look at each other

we agree it's a good idea

we take the cranes off the string and
    open their wings to release them

Thank you, Students Rebuild!

it is nice to think of others
            faraway
            helping

we will send them the first week of April
  to make the deadline

no afternoon chime calls children home
we have lost track of time

Yuka's mother calls her home

with plans to meet tomorrow
Yuka takes home half of the

❦ ❦ ❦

I fold press release
through the news

concern about radiation is growing

18:41 even stronger

18:49

I fold press release
after dinner and
through

18:53 shock

19:31 after

19:43 shock

20:06

22:27

Father makes it back, and
sleepwalks through to bed

he is going to the office
    working
    doing his part
like others in Japan

to keep "the money going around"
to carry on

to keep Japan strong

22:31 the house pushes up then
sideways

we all meet under the table

TV tells us it was south
strong and shallow

under Mount Fuji

!!!!!

that's down here

closer to west Tokyo
than the one on March 11

experts have expected Mount Fuji to erupt someday

with "The Big One"

maybe someday
soon?

Earth responds with

22:35 a nudge from up north
22:37 a stronger one

22:40 weaker
22:40 stronger
22:43 weaker

in the stillness
alone in my room

I unpack the glow-in-the-dark emergency ladder
  open the window
  loop its end around the window box rail
  push it over the edge and
  watch it unravel

the end of the rope and metal rungs
hit the ground with a thud and a clunk

this was the drill
Mother and Father showed me
when I was five
it seemed like a long way down

before I get under the covers
I line all the cranes I've made
along my windowsill
counting them one by one by one

35 CRANES

it's a long way to one thousand

DAY 6

02:40

04:53

05:30

06:04

the telephone rings early
no sixth-grade graduation tomorrow—
it is delayed until further notice

I watch Father leave at his usual time

the bright ladder catches his eye
he looks up at me in the window

you're prepared, I hear him say

we wave
before he slowly starts on his way to the station

his bag weighs him down

08:58

9:22 WOW!
Mother grabs her laptop
I grab my mug
we scramble under the table

Mother checks the location of the quake
on the Japan Meteorological Agency website
to see how close it was
then
she goes to the quake map and
clicks to watch from March 11

circles flash by time order
widen by magnitude, and
brighten by depth

why relive it?

The emperor of Japan gives a rare appearance
on TV

in a prerecorded speech

he expresses sadness for the people of the Northeast

he says we will keep thinking of those affected
and will work to rebuild

he worries about the radiation
and asks us to
be united and
take care of one another

on TV
experts report radiation levels are above normal

but safe

in a video
experts explain radiation to children saying
the nuclear energy plant is Nuclear Boy,
a baby with a stomachache

the worst-case scenario is a soiled diaper

no one knows how to dispose of it

now the baby is only farting
and the people closest to him are affected

online
people down here are saying

we should stay indoors
          close windows
          make the house airtight
          hang laundry inside
          avoid breathing bad air

what air will we breathe?

grit sits on every windowsill in this house
we cannot keep the fields out

how can we stop radiation?

foreigners are leaving Japan
they are returning to their home countries

they feel it is unsafe here and
it is time to go

Mother is losing her clients
her work
her income

from my window
I see
Grandmother watching the daffodils
waving at me then
heading for the vegetable stand

the wind is blowing
I watch the daffodils dance

we learned in school
that
these golden flowers protect themselves

rooted
they turn their heads
away from the wind

rooted
they twist
so they do not break

rooted
they dance
in the wind

we are fortunate

down here

the direction of the wind has shifted
  from the Northeast

❦ ❦ ❦

the doorbell rings
a deliveryman
arrives with a package special express
of
slender whistles on strings
from Father
with a note

"please wear"

he must be losing confidence in the house

Mother and I go out into shifted winds
to give one each to Grandmother and Great-grandfather

Great-grandfather puts it to his lips
                    blows

TTT—WWWEEEE—TTTT

                    asks if it's a dog whistle

it's not only for rescue dogs, we tell him

can we count on him?

no matter what
we will save each other
or
neighbors will come to dig us out
of the rubble

neighbors who built homes
on land Great-great grandfather bought
and sold plot by plot
for money
to send Grandfather and Father
to university

this land holds
artifacts
underneath

the city restricts digging to a certain depth
in this area

archeologists came in
before the land was broken
for the one-stop shop

at its grand opening,
some very old pots were displayed

what happened to all the people?
why did they leave those pots?

12:52
12:53
12:55

❦ ❦ ❦

Yuka cannot come over
to fold cranes

Dear People of the Northeast!

Everyone is worried about radiation.
Some people won't go outside down here.
How scared you must be up there closer to the leak!

from Maya 💔

13:14

13:17

I sit across from Mother
and

each time I fold
                press
                release

I think of the girl
we all learn about in elementary school

the girl
folding cranes
after
becoming sick from radiation
from the atomic bomb in Hiroshima
in World War II

with each fold
I am wishing for everyone's health

I ask to use Mother's laptop

I search

"clean up radiation"

a photo
catches my eye

a sunflower

I read
"experiments show
sunflowers can drink
low levels of radiation from soil"

can a flower clean up Earth?

we need to plant some

lots

and
I know
where
I can get sunflower seeds

Yuka's grandmother plants them
collects their seeds
replants them
every year

I've seen Yuka's photos of her garden and
her never-ending cycle
of

sunflowers!

I join Great-grandfather and Grandmother
at the vegetable stand
for their tea break

I tell them about sunflowers and
  ask if I can plant some to collect the seeds
                                             to send to the Northeast

I say,
I really wish I had a field of sunflowers
even though
I know
they plan to plant more vegetables
for a Japanese relief group

Great-grandfather suggests planting a corner
                                   of sunflowers

he hears well enough for important things

he hands me the hoe and
    heads out to the fields

I follow behind

he shows me where to start
                how to strike and
                how deep to go

the ground is not that hard

it's been tilled
            turned and
            loosened
through the seasons

I strike
  turn
  loosen
  move forward and
  strike
          along the edge of
                the corner

I prepare
for sunflowers

one row
ready to sow
energizes me

I keep going

18:15

in the evening
I am so tired I cannot move
20:20 even when Earth shudders

and

21:02 shakes
so close (east of Tokyo in the sea)
so shallow
and

22:39 so strong

25 CRANES

DAY 7

02:19

07:05

a letter arrives from Principal
an apology
for the delay of the sixth graders' graduation

"it cannot be helped"
(the gym is under inspection and repair)

she looks forward to meeting many of us under the
  cherry blossoms
                    to wish the sixth graders well
at an informal ceremony with their parents
on April 5
and then
on April 6
for the first day of school

she also gives encouragement for the days ahead

I find a text from Yuka
saying she and her mother are on their way
south to her grandparents'
until school starts

I am crushed
I have always counted on Yuka
to be here

it's brave to leave home
they could get stuck somewhere
along the way
in "The Big One"

I text her
asking about cranes
and
asking for sunflowers seeds
telling her to be careful

I wait for a response
but my text is "unread"

out in the fields
I strike
  turn
  loosen soil
in the corner for sunflowers

it's a cold day
hoeing doesn't warm me up
I go inside for lunch
the text I sent Yuka is still "unread"

13:10 the house shakes me

I return to the table to fold cranes

sunshine floods the dining room
but I cannot get warm
in the house

Dear People of the Northeast!

My best friend left. The weather is like winter. I am under blankets in my own home and still feel cold. I want to tell you not to lose heart, but it is worse for you. I think you must know better comforting words than I do.

from Maya

the kerosene truck hasn't been
circling
the neighborhood
blasting
"Around the World in 80 Days"
filling
heater tanks

maybe there is a shortage
maybe it is all sent up north
it's the end of the season
but it's cold
it must be so cold up there

to warm ourselves usually
we would take a hot bath
but to fill the tub
would take time and
                    energy to heat the water

we could end up with an empty tub or
                              caught in the tub
when
15:24 Earth moves

a bath is a luxury

but some people
here
and
there
don't want to be anywhere near water

we keep the electric pot filled
for tea
but later

17:25

clank! clank! clank!

makes me

21:02

21:32 colder

21:33

21:54

before going to bed
I warm myself
looking at photos
of
sunflowers

22:37

40 CRANES

DAY 8

00:51

01:44 Earth pushes
wakes me

03:55 I'm rocked
back to sleep

still no text from Yuka

the house is so cold I stay under blankets

I hear Mother tell Father
an embassy e-mail says
the US government is evacuating American citizens
from Tokyo to East Asia

Father tells her we can go

I hear her say,

we cannot go

this is home

she is plugged in
working at her laptop
communicating with and
helping out
foreigners who are leaving

from my window
I see Grandmother heading to the vegetable stand

Great-grandfather is sowing seeds for more vegetables

before Father leaves the house
he comes, stands beside me
asks if I want to leave

I know Mother would go if I wanted
I know he would let us go
they would let me go

I look at him
then out
at Grandmother and Great-grandfather
in the fields

and tell him, *no*

out in the fields
I watch

09:41 Earth shake the house
our home

I look up

where are you *going?*
I ask passing clouds

I look down
on the row I hoed
take my shoes off
and
curl my toes deep
past the topsoil
into warmth

Great-grandfather looks at my bare feet and
says nothing

the slim rubber soles of
his *jikatabi*
keep him close to the ground
stable

silk braids
from old floor mats
dangle from his belt

he ties poles together
crisscrossed
two by two
to support

young bean plants

he gently directs these tender vines

to the poles

I follow behind him
but
do not ask to help

he has his own rhythm

I reach out to a straggler he missed
and
  notice a shadow walking
along the edge of the park fence

a black cat wearing a red collar
                    sits down and watches me

later
I check my phone
still my text is "unread"
I'm worried about Yuka

Mother says, *traveling takes longer now*

I fold
  press
  release several cranes and
  notice

at our dining room sliding glass door
the black cat is watching me

I open the door to shoo it away

the cat steps inside
            sits and
            looks up at me

do you know this cat? Mother asks

no

she tries to coax the cat outside

17:01 the house shakes

the collar bell dings

the cat sits
shifts
settles

Mother checks the collar
no tag
no name
no contact information

we have no idea who this cat is

I'll call the vet tomorrow

Mother bikes to 7-Eleven to buy cat food and litter
buys the last bags on the shelf
makes a litter box out of a vegetable tray
a bed out of a cardboard box and
a flyer with the cat's picture on it

I make a flyer
asking for sunflower seed donations

the cat sits in front of

17:16 me under the table

17:27 watching

and at bedtime
follows me to my room

23:10

and sits at a distance
in the dark

this cat must think I rescued it

I only opened the door

25 CRANES

DAY 9

1:49

04:53

06:18

up early for Saturday
Father stops on his way to the kitchen
    says, *eh-h-h-h?*
when he
    sees the cat
sitting beside me at the table

Mother explains

Father smiles
    says, *really?*

I ignore the conversation

we have a cat, Father says
when he sees the litter box, bed, and bowls

Mother calls the vet
            tells us he doesn't know about
                                    a missing black cat
            says we'll go for a checkup this afternoon

I ignore the conversation

this cat creates more work, more worry

he has come

08:32 at the wrong time

Father takes a copy of Mother's flyer
out to the vegetable stand
I follow with the flyer I made

the cat will not follow me outside

Father joins Great-grandfather
to dig up young leeks
to transplant them in deeper trenches
to protect them
and
to give them room
to reach deep and grow long

the starling pecks through the trenches

I take off my shoes

barefoot
I join them

the sun makes me
take off my windbreaker

we work side by side by side

08:49 Earth jolts us

08:50 but we are in Great-grandfather's rhythm
like clockwork
we finish the job

at the garden sink
Father says nothing about my feet

he only says, *this dirt never washes off completely*

❦ ❦ ❦

Father looks happy to return to the fields
after lunch
Mother asks me to walk
to the animal clinic
beside her bicycle
with the cat in the basket
(she tempted him with fish)

I do not want to go
but go
to stop by the hardware shop
afterward

at the clinic
the vet puts Mother's flyer in the window
thanks us for fostering him
(it's a boy)
gives us samples of food and litter
(cats can be picky)
says he hasn't been out long, and

adds,

this cat was loved

at the hardware shop
Goto-san greets us

I scan the racks for sunflower seeds
don't see them and
ask

Goto-san tells me, not in yet
                                        not to worry
                                        there's time
                                        next month is the time to plant here

the cat watches me come out

he almost looks sad for me

as I fold cranes
Mother tells me
she knows about cats

as a kid
she went from house to house
some had cats

she moved on but the cats stayed

cats can be good friends

she spends the afternoon making the cat feel at home

the table is off limits
but he doesn't understand

Mother starts calling him "Shadow"
in English

he is attached to me but
    is never too near

always watching me

I watch the pendant light
checking to see if it's moving
        to see if Earth's moving

I cannot tell

it feels like we are always moving

I fold press release

Shadow watches from a distance

at dinner
I don't need to check the light
18:56 I grab my mug and
    head under the table

Shadow is still

watching me

I hear Father in their bedroom
snoring
snorting
snoozing soundly

field work is good for me, he tells us
before going to bed early

Shadow follows me to bed
watches me count cranes on my windowsill
watches me turn out the light

the supermoon
in
Shadow's eyes
is the last thing

I see

25 CRANES

DAY 10

in the morning
Shadow is the first thing I see

he wants to be fed

it's my chore
along with cleaning his litter box

Mother heads out on her bike

Father and Grandmother set up the vegetable stand
I go out to the fields to join Great-grandfather

looking back at the house
I see Shadow sitting on my windowsill

10:30 crushing my cranes

a man parks his bike at the edge of the field
walks out
stands in front of a cabbage head
motions to Great-grandfather and
asks to buy it

Great-grandfather says it is not good quality
says it is last season's
the man insists

Great-grandfather nudges it
slides his knife underneath
between it and Earth

he rolls it from hand to hand
inspects it
pulls outer leaves away
lets them fall and
hands it to the man
telling him to pay Grandmother at the vegetable stand

I follow him

the man asks Grandmother to cut it in half
to fit in his bicycle basket

the cabbage crunches open
beneath her knife
exposing
a Fibonacci swirl of leaves

folding
leaf over leaf
holding
months of air, water, sun
from this field
before the radiation scare

good to have one from here
the man says, and

buys spinach and leeks too

the sky darkens
I go inside
14:58 the house shifts with a strong
shallow
shake

Dear People of the Northeast,

I wish we had fresh vegetables to send you.
Someday I hope I have sunflower seeds for you.

from Maya

I fold
press
release

later
I overhear Mother and Father
discussing
Tokyo city water

it is unsafe for babies

radiation levels are too high for babies

leaks are still not under control
the one-stop shop already limits water purchases

what happens when everyone needs bottled water?

Dear People of the Northeast,

I keep hoping the nuclear energy company knows what to do.

from Maya 💔

Earth has been still for hours
then

23:48 I roll off my bed and
slide under my desk

I hear Shadow's bell
come closer
in the darkness

25 CRANES

DAY 11

00:06

04:54

05:05

Father leaves home well rested
Mother works at the table
I watch raindrops in garden puddles

they look like the phantom circles
of aftershocks
on the quake map

ding

Yuka texts 

sorry took longer
hard to text from here

she's down south
in the countryside

Yuka is lucky
she's on stable ground and
in sunshine

inside this house
is colder than outside

Shadow is lucky
he's wearing a fur coat

I feel lucky to hear Yuka's okay
I don't mind she didn't answer my questions

Grandmother stops by on her way
to the family grave
for the spring equinox visit and

says I should not go

caution, not fear

people have been injured by
stones falling at temples and graveyards

I will go another time
to scrub the headstones
place flowers
and burn incense

I am hoping Grandmother
will be

14:08 okay

Dear People of the Northeast,

Today, Grandmother went alone to our family grave. Every day for two years, I have been missing my grandfather. Today they are saying over twenty thousand people are dead or missing because of the earthquake and tsunami!!

That means many thousands of people are sad and worried. Some dead people have no surviving family members to take care of their remains and there is not enough fuel up there for cremation. They cannot bury the dead in the proper way. Old grave sites have been washed away too. It's so sad.

I am wishing everyone will rest in peace.

from Maya 

I run to meet Grandmother at our gates
see she is okay and
throw salt on her
front and back
to make sure no ghosts followed her home

she brings back *botamochi* for teatime
cautions me
not to let the cat get any

it's sticky
messy and
dangerous for pets

I tell her,
he sits on the table
but never bothers anything

after dinner I fold cranes

19:43 I grab paper
my mug
and
dart under the table

Shadow jumps down
sits in front of me
slowly blinking at me

I wonder if he is finally freaking out
but then he stops

I tell Mother,
there's something wrong with his eyes

she observes him
that's how cats show affection

a cup of hot tea and a sweet
welcome Father home

he sighs
    sits
    says, *good eh?*

Mother joins him

Shadow follows me to my room

22:49 we are shaken

would Shadow follow me down the ladder?

I don't think I can rescue him

50 CRANES

DAY 12

00:27

12:31
12:38
12:41
12:56

13:12
13:15
13:44

Dear People of the Northeast!

Aftershocks are shallow and close.
And more rain today!
I wish you sunny skies. It is harder to be strong in rain.
The sun makes the days better.

from Maya

I fold press and release
a crane

Shadow swats at it

no!

I release another

Shadow swats at it

no!

and another

three cranes sit
wing to wing to wing

Shadow swats at them
a claw catches hold of one

it flies

he pounces
after it

drops onto it

slashing claws
gnashing teeth
the crane is in shreds

no!

I shout at, charge at, chase after him

he darts to the entry hall
barrels past Mother

out into the rain

Mother says, *he needs a toy*

she finds a string and ties it to a chopstick
but he doesn't come back

I look up
          away
          from the table

Shadow sits at the door
Mother lets him in
out of the rain

I am not happy with him
but do not scold him

Mother is worried
his fur coat is sopping wet

she feels she needs to use the hair dryer
      hesitates
but
      insists it
needs to be done

she sits at a distance blow-drying his fur

a rattle
a rumble
a shake

16:18 we dash under the table
16:18 !!!
two aftershocks
within seconds of each other

Shadow moves in front of me
sits closer than ever to me
calmly

17:33
I realize
18:19 he's been watching over me
18:44

we go to bed early
to conserve solar batteries

21:04 I lie in bed

22:50 wondering if I will need the ladder

I cannot see Shadow
but I feel his presence
and
hear his bell

25 CRANES

DAY 13

00:03
01:12

07:12
07:34
07:34

Father packs his umbrella
the forecast is rain in the afternoon

07:53

by this time in March
I would be on school break

we left suddenly
        everything undone
        everything unfinished
        everything left behind

there is no homework
        no assignment
        no project
        no cram school
        no English practice

I have all the time in the world

to think and worry

❦ ❦ ❦

Dear People of the Northeast,

The government banned milk and some vegetables from farms near the nuclear energy plant. Experts still say radiation levels are safe but not if you drink or eat a lot of these things. Poor farmers and cows! And the poor people who live nearby. They have low levels of radiation too.

I wish this problem was finished.

from Maya 💔

Shadow watches me fold

he does not make a move
but
to protect all of my cranes
I gather them
together
                to string them
together

they will be stronger

sliding one onto the back
of another
then another
then another

1, 2, 3 . . . 10 cranes
1, 2, 3 . . . another 10
1, 2, 3 . . . another 10

Mother reaches out to help
glances at the chains of cranes, asks,
there's an order?

my fingers
my hands
my brain
have found an order

by color or design
and
by number

but I tell her,
not really
anything is okay

Shadow pats the air near the end of the chain

don't you dare

Mother tries to get him interested in the toy she made

he is not interested

she ties the shredded crane to the end of the string

give him his own so he's not tempted, she says

it works

he plays
    rests
then
    sits beside me

19:43 blinking

still

21:19 blinking

20 CRANES

DAY 14

05:28
05:32
05:43

work life continues

Father leaves for the office
Mother leaves for relief centers

08:48

so cold and cloudy
I stay at the table

08:56 or under it

in the mailbox
I am so happy to see
an envelope from Yuka

tucked inside a folded paper conceals
                    a seed
                    a sunflower seed
a note says
she will bring more and
          help me plant them before school starts

clutching the seed
I imagine
these cheerful golden flowers

in Great-grandfather's field

tracking the sun
cleansing Earth
brightening us

I place the seed in front of me
as I fold cranes

Shadow pats at the seed

I shoo him

he bolts

my mug is airborne

I reach out

no!

tea splatters

the mug hits the wooden floor

one shard breaks off
                    lands near the whole

I cradle the piece into the other

shocked
and sad
no tears come for this broken gift

I shout,
nothing in this house
broke
in the big quake

and then you come

you mess things up!

I dab the floor with a tea towel

Shadow sits by the door
wanting outside
for the first time
since he came inside

I let him out
not wanting to see him again

12:58 I am

14:03 alone

17:20 Shadow's not here

21:06 and stays gone

25 CRANES

DAY 15

02:08

04:17

07:07 a nudge from the south

is Earth spinning?
I cannot tell

is the ground moving?
the pendant light and the quake map say *no*

my head is full of swirls

I open the door
on my way out to the fields

Grandmother is there
holding Shadow

she says he was restless all night

Shadow jumps from her arms
and heads to the gate
I ask her to come inside

I show her my mug

this can be repaired, she says

I follow her to the shed
Shadow follows too, but
does not step inside

he stands at the door

Grandmother digs past tools
looking for a box
with materials to repair
a broken dish
with gold

she gives me an overview
of what she learned

I hesitate, saying, *but . . .*

she says,
better for you to repair it

but

step by step

first step—
file jagged edges
to deepen and widen
the crack
so
resin will hold

she shows me
    watches me
    steps back

this is how she taught me to make cranes
as a preschooler

showing me
step by step

watching me
step by step

leaving me
alone with the paper

but being present with encouragement

under her watchful eye
I file
the broken pieces

she praises my work

Shadow watches from the door

we break for lunch

before we part
she invites me in to see
her favorite white teacup
she repaired
many years ago

my fingers glide over the gold splintered lines

a plum branch, we say together

I am a part of the history of this teacup

I was the one standing at the shed door

I don't remember Grandmother being mad at me

later
Shadow sits at the shed door
Grandmother slides open a window
wind whips through

we snap on plastic gloves

she uncaps the jar of resin
    dips out a portion
    taps it onto a cardboard square
    drips water droplets
    over it
    mixing and releasing
    a smell that sickens me
    takes my breath away
    makes my head spin
I hold my breath then
  breathe
  in
  out
  in
  out
  through my mouth

she brushes a dab onto an edge then
    hands me the brush

careful

lacquer resin blisters skin

I brush resin
onto edges

and fit the pieces together

the mug will rest with wet towels inside a box
for a week

a week?

it takes time, she says

but Earth . . .

she tells me,
you will start over again
bringing the pieces together
until they hold

I walk out to the fields
Shadow follows

I breathe easily again

Great-grandfather unfolds plastic
to cover a seeded row

I take one end

the wind catches it
the starling flies up from behind

oh!

he flies away
but
he will come back
to find a way under the plastic

17:45

Shadow does not show up for dinner

20:36 he is gone

20 CRANES

DAY 16

Mother boils kelp
for iodine
to drink
even though
they're saying radiation levels are okay down here

she signs up for iodine pills through the US Embassy
in case things get worse

Father wakes up happy
his day off is sunny

but after breakfast
instead of going out to the fields
he decides to go off with Mother
to help her
gather and donate

I go out to check the mug

Shadow is sitting
at the shed entrance

at his feet
the starling lies

limp, lifeless

dead!

an earth-shattering cry rises
from my rib cage

a cry worthy for
the last bird on Earth

Great-grandfather hears it
comes running
sees what has happened
takes a breath

and says, *that's a cat*

Great-grandfather suggests letting Shadow have the starling

sees my shattered face then
shows me a place at the wall
where the field meets the garden

Shadow follows us

Great-grandfather helps me bury the bird

we bow our heads
in silent prayer

he gathers his tools
and heads out into the field

I follow
and sit
looking out to birdless fields

later
Father joins Great-grandfather in the fields
works until sunset

19:18

falls asleep early

19:42

from the sliding door
Shadow watches me

fold cranes

Mother lets him in
says she doesn't know but thinks
the bird was a gift

—but—

that cannot fix anything

40 CRANES

DAY 17

04:52

I am not happy Shadow is in the house
he will not go outside

he knows I won't let him back in

I go out

in the shed
I open the box

the broken piece has shifted
out from the mug

the resin is soft enough
to ease it gently
back into place

I pack it away
I stay away from the house
and
join Father and Great-grandfather
in the fields

12:20

I work all afternoon in the field

after tea and dinner
19:23 I stay at the table

Shadow keeps an eye on me
I keep an eye on him
while I fold cranes

Mother says he is happy here
he has stayed
because he likes me

he is a house cat
and doesn't belong outside

I don't ask why no one has come for him
I think I know the answer

Mother tells me,
you are saving his life

22:41 the shudder
of Shadow's bell
makes me teary-eyed

20 CRANES

DAY 18

06:11

07:23
07:23

Great-grandfather loosens baby spinach plants
one by one
from their bed

placing them in a bamboo basket

he transplants them
to give them room

I watch him
remembering the day
Shadow watched me
followed me home
wanted inside
never wanting outside

I step behind Great-grandfather
and
pat the soil snugly around the baby spinach roots

all day out
we miss a call from the vet

the message says he has some news
but gives no details

Shadow may be going home!

19:40

30 CRANES

DAY 19

08:01

Grandmother asks me to wash and prepare
leeks and some of the baby spinach
to set out at the vegetable stand

I wash and wash and wash

she tells me, *everyone expects some grit*
it cannot be helped

my flyer still hangs on the post
even though no one has seeds and
no one mentions it anymore

the flyer for Shadow is gone

this may be Shadow's last day
at our house

Great-grandfather tills the broccoli stalks
into the ground
alone
no starling follows him

I walk out farther to the park
to the cherry buds
tightly closed

our neighborhood blossom-viewing is canceled
many across Tokyo, too

out of respect for the losses up north

before dinner
Mother tells me
there's no word from the vet yet
he was in surgery all day

I ask to use her laptop
to look up planting times for sunflowers

I look further and
learn
a Japanese scientist is working on
how to dispose
of their stalks after they absorb radiation

sunflowers are not the answer

19:54 I end up under the table

will radiation ever go away?

30 CRANES

DAY 20

Mother places the flyer she made
for Shadow on the table

the vet called to say

a neighbor of Shadow's guardian
saw the photo in his window
and
told him
the woman's grandson chased Shadow out
after she died

I ask,
what is his real name?

the neighbor didn't know

my heart softens more for him

17:52

he has lost his guardian
his home
his name

he has nowhere to go

I write "Shadow" at the top of the flyer
cross out "Contact" and
write "HOME" next to our information

I give Shadow a slow blink

Mother says I have rescued him

21:51 Shadow jumps up on my bed

the rumble deep
beneath his heart
lulls me to sleep

22:19

25 CRANES

DAY 21

8:52

my mug is ready for gold dust

with Grandmother standing near

I rub the seam
first with fine charcoal grit
to smooth rough spots

then with a fine brush

I tap gold powder onto a paper square

with cotton fluff
I dab along the seam
inside and
outside
the mug

it needs to sit
undisturbed for a week

12:25 if
16:15 possible

Shadow follows me to the shed to check on the mug

he follows me everywhere
inside and
outside

20 CRANES

DAY 22

I will join Mother
to search for donations for the Northeast

on my first train ride
after March 11

she advises packing my water bottle
                                        my emergency weather cape
in case we have to walk home

and my whistle
in case . . .

the station is dimly lit
escalators and elevators are halted

sitting on the train
my stomach churns with possibilities
of things that could happen
if "The Big One" happens

caution, not fear
I remember Grandmother saying

we choose not to go too far
from home

we stop along the train line
going to different shops
looking for toilet paper, soap, slippers
and
gathering other things on her list
to drop off to send to evacuation centers

I see
"origami paper" on her list and
remind her to buy kitty litter

on our way into the gate
Mother thanks me for helping

I apologize for not helping sooner

but you have been helping, she says

we stop to watch
our porch swallows
inspect their nesting spot
preparing to return later

for the first clutch of eggs

Shadow must stay in the house
or use the back door

especially when the fledglings are learning to fly

20:57

he watches me
fold
my very last crane

I didn't shout once

I thank him for cooperating

20 CRANES

DAY 23

from my window I see Yuka
passing under the cherry tree
on her way to my house

she's holding a plastic bag
lit by the sun
filled with colors of the rainbow

through the house
                    gate
                    street
I run

we grab hands
    lean in and
    smile into each other's faces

she places a bag
                the size of a clenched fist and
                the weight of one paper crane
filled with sunflower seeds
into my hand

I tell her I prepared
a corner for sunflowers in Great-grandfather's fields

we will plant them
after we send the cranes

Yuka meets Shadow

she understands why I strung the cranes
(her grandmother used to have a cat)

one thousand cranes
require a big box

Mother has two
just right

14:08 the table wobbles

Yuka panics
rushes under it
Shadow and I join her

I get a piece of origami paper and write:

Dear People of the Northeast,

Yuka and I will grow sunflowers in Great-grandfather's field.

We will gather and send you seeds.

from Maya and Yuka 💔

Yuka signs it
folds
presses
releases

a flying crane

I ask her to add it to her box

Shadow watches

Yuka and I stack
pack and
address two boxes
to post

1,001 cranes

on Monday

the neighborhood chime calls
her home

before she leaves
16:55 she heads under the table

18:05
19:22

after dinner
Mother asks me to take care of dinner dishes
it's her turn to join the fire group

there is no blackout
no emergency candles in use
but it is a cold night
people may use their heaters

and Earth may move

I ask to go
we leave the dishes
say *good-bye and be good* to Shadow and
tell Grandmother where we're going

at the park
we greet neighbors

it feels warm and cozy
to see people out
together

the blocks are handed out
Mother hands me her set

we start out
they clank
I don't

clank! clank!
watch out for fire!

up close
the hollow clank is startling

we walk along

I am out of step
I try but
I am out of sync

clank! clank! clank! clank!
watch watch out out for for fire! fire!

in a few more steps I am with the group

clank! clank!
watch out for fire!

DAY 24

02:07

Sunday
under sunless skies
out on the edge and
in the corner
where I prepared the soil for sunflowers

I take off my shoes

Yuka giggles
surprised by my earth-stained feet

Great-grandfather is with us
on his day off
if we need him

together
side by side
shoulder to shoulder
seed by seed
Yuka and I poke a hole
cover the seed and
pat the earth
we fill the corner
and a bit beyond

we have seeds left over

11:49 Yuka steadies herself on my arm

she tells me
we may have
to support the seedlings
until they are strong enough
to stand on their own

side by side
we look out where
they will stand
side by side
along a corner
of the field

a future golden summer angle

how many days until sunflower seeds?
Yuka says, *who knows?*

a new count begins

16:38

21:43

22:18

THIS IS **DAY 1 ASP** (AFTER SUNFLOWER PLANTING)

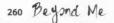

DAY 2 ASP

walking
we head into the wind
hugging the boxes tight

any lift and
they will be airborne

stopping
we watch Great-grandfather dig up
his vault of taro tubers
kept underground through winter

he has already softened the soil by hoe
to plant them

we turn a corner

the wind at our backs
pushes us along

the air is clean and clear

neither of us mentions radiation levels

we send the cranes airmail to America and
the extra seeds to the scientist for his experiments

returning
we check the sunflower bed

on a far corner
Great-grandfather tucks baby taro
into a shallow bed

they will raise
a small leaf or two
asking to be moved
to a deeper bed
with a heavier blanket of soil

in summer
the leaves will bow and wave
as we pass
to and from school

we check the sakura tree at the park
some buds are opening

we wonder if

our school yard tree will be in bloom
when fifth graders meet to sing to the sixth graders
tomorrow

after they give us rice seeds for next year's project

20:46

DAY 3 ASP

04:30
05:43

Yuka and I arrive early
we go out and
take our time under the cherry tree

the tree is late
not in full bloom
but
blossoms are opening

parents arriving early
amble around before taking a chair
holding their breath
not mentioning how late
the cherry blossoms are

no student
no mother
no grandparent is wearing spring colors

fathers wear businessman suits
like always

inside

at our desks
in our last year's classroom
with last year's teacher
we sing the song Teacher chose
for the choir concert

life is mysterious . . .

the thrush
high in mulberry branches
joins us

. . . love rushes in . . .

we are out of sync
    all over the place
    out of tune
but we carry on

life is a glorious thing

it makes my heart ring

at our appointed time
we fifth graders file
onto the playground

class by class
we line up shoulder to shoulder
to stand in front of a sixth-grade class

each student reaches out
to hand each of us
a handmade envelope of rice seeds

I wish we had enough sunflower seeds to give them

under the cherry tree
we gather to sing
Moriyama's biggest hit
we practiced weeks ago

I'm sure we are waiting . . .

everyone
students
parents
grandparents know it and
join us in the chorus
softly
gently
sadly

sakura sakura

some choke on,
now in bloom

we finish the song together

tomorrow they will be seventh graders
tomorrow we will be sixth graders

endings and beginnings are tearful

this year especially

13:32

18:08

after dinner
I sing Teacher's choice to
Grandmother
Great-grandfather
Mother and
Father (he came home early to hear me)

they join in
    shed tears and
    say they are happy
        they didn't miss it

23:41

DAY 3 ASP

first day of sixth grade for me
a half day
with no lunch service
like always

same teacher
same classmates

new classroom
new textbooks
new notebooks

no one is happy to be back

how sad the first day of school
must be
for the people of the Northeast

we share our stories
our fears
our hopes

we pledge to find ways to help

first step—

we write a postcard to children in the affected area

Dear People of the Northeast,

I hope you have felt the love rushing in from us and people around Japan and the world. My broken heart is filled with hope for you.

from Maya ♥

I uncover my mug
brush away excess gold
hold it up to show Grandmother

she asks me
if I see
anything

in the repair

my heart healing

at the vegetable stand
customers comment on nuclear energy

some mention
America's Three Mile Island
the Soviet Union's Chernobyl

everyone mentions what's happening here
using the company's name

not the place

for the disaster

some mention our disaster is not as bad as the others
based on the radiation levels listed
in the media

we get by with fewer lights at home
at school
at shops
at stations
on streets

everywhere

I wonder why

do we need all of them?

19:09

21:56

22:54

DAY 4 ASP

at school in class

11:40 aftershocks

12:16 happen

we follow rules
and carry on

at home in bed

23:32 Earth rocks us
I respond with caution
not (much) fear

and go back to sleep
with Shadow's purr

DAY 7 ASP

cherry blossoms bloom

there are no parties, no picnics

we view them with quiet appreciation
and watch as

new green follows

sprouts rise from the sunflower bed

we cover them
to keep birds from eating them and
rain from beating them

we look forward

to seeds

DAY 9 ASP

THE ONE-MONTH ANNIVERSARY OF MARCH 11

02:44
06:35 Earth
08:47

13:51 reminds us to follow rules

17:16 and
17:17 keeps
17:19
17:20
17:26 reminding
17:33
17:45
17:58
17:59

18:05 us
18:06
18:12
18:30
18:36
19:00 throughout the evening
20:27
20:42 about what happened a month ago
22:05

we count

22 aftershocks

DAY 10 ASP

00:21

00:57

at breakfast

08:08 one aftershock

then

08:13 another one

much more than a swirl

at school

08:48 we move under our desks

11:23 with our emergency hoods on

14:07 again we're up and under

14:10 back

and

14:26 forth

17:48

I count

10 aftershocks

today

BY DAY 28 ASP

Grandfather's clock keeps time

we are all back on schedule

the lone pine
the miracle tree
gives hope and inspiration
for the nation
even through the threat of storms

signs everywhere say
Carry On

up north
recovery is slow
people live in temporary housing

radiation levels threaten some areas

the nuclear company struggles to know what to do

Japanese scientists
a Buddhist priest
and groups
each ask the public
for sunflower seeds

to plant in the affected areas of Japan

the news tells us
radiation levels remain low

we do what we can to carry on

we put money in donation boxes at shops
and
take goods to drop-off points

Yuka and I brace our young sunflowers
with a windbreak of poles and old *tatami* braids
to protect them from
summer rains and typhoon winds

we find out
Students Rebuild received two million cranes
for Japan

some cranes
will come back here

to make a work of art
for the people of the Northeast

maybe our cranes will return to Japan

BY DAY 79 ASP

Earth still moves at least once every day

Prime Minister Kan shut down a nuclear plant
near a fault line

people here
and there
march with signs

No nukes!
Protect the children!
Save Earth!

DAY 113 ASP

up there
people still need help
workers still struggle at the nuclear plant
officials still say we are safe

down here
Great-grandfather's field is full of
sound and movement

crows squawk
starlings shriek
cicadas screech

heart-shaped taro leaves
as big as elephant ears
and
taller than Yuka and me
nod
bob
bow

golden-petaled sunflowers
as tall as we are
reach
shift
sway

bees buzz
zip
sip
east-facing flowers

swallows dive
dip
nip
high-flying insects

dragonflies dart
dash
clip
all-flying insects

I watch dragonflies maneuver

each glimmering wing whirls the air

these ancient pilots
were on Earth before dinosaurs

will they survive us too?

Yuka and I
lean into sunflower faces
breathe their sweet perfume and
count
lose count
re-count their young seeds in
clockwise and counterclockwise
swirls

something bigger than a bee hums
                   hovers
                   darts
from flower to flower

hoshihōjaku, a kind of moth,
Yuka tells me
looks icky and cute at the same time

she sees them in her grandmother's garden

I tell her about hummingbirds

how they hum
          hover and
          dart
like
this moth

how their colors sparkle
                    brighten
                    change with each movement
                                        each flutter
                                        each breath
not like
this moth

but
this moth

matches sunflower colors!

we watch him until he flies away
    then
    begin the count again
    lose count
    re-count

we are eager to harvest

Shadow follows me everywhere
        watches over me

and the sunflowers

he keeps birds away from the seeds
I keep him away from the birds

we hope we have many to pass along

we hope
they will someday help scientists learn how

to repair Earth

now
the fields are overflowing
with vegetables

the vegetable stand is overflowing
with customers

the one-stop shop is overflowing
with local farm vegetables
in a narrow section

ours are among them and
among donations trucked north

Father talks about quitting his job
to farm

I quit cram school and no longer
study for a top junior high school

I spend time in the fields
helping

it keeps me on my toes

13:34 even when Earth moves
below me

they say we will have aftershocks for years
along with other earthquakes too

who knows when Tokyo's Big One will come?

we carry on
            taking care of what is in front of us
            taking care of ourselves
            taking care of those who need help

I stay grounded in the folded
                        the rooted
                        the winged
                        the mended
                        the seeded
                        the needed

and the belled

my mug
holds together

with lacquer and gold dust

it is more beautiful
and stronger than before

it fell to the floor again and

it did not break

I can trust its mended cracks
but
I found another use for it

AUTHOR'S NOTE

The Great East Japan Earthquake and Tsunami on March 11, 2011 left us many stories. Hopefully there will be books and translations from the most affected areas. I chose to tell a story close to home.

Home alone in west Tokyo, I saw, heard, and felt all the boards of our wooden house jolt and groan. Earth rocked us minutes, hours, days, and weeks afterwards. Many foreign residents evacuated because of concern about the damage of the nuclear energy plant in the Northeast and concern about the big earthquake that experts say will devastate Tokyo.

I am a foreign resident. Papa is a Japanese citizen. Our children are American and Japanese. We did not want to leave. We have roots here. We lived with Aunt and Grandmother. One child was preparing to go to the United States for university in June. The other was finishing junior high and would start high school in April, down close to Tokyo Bay. We had dogs and cats. How could we leave and come back?

Earth kept shaking, and when it wasn't shaking we thought it was shaking. This "earthquake sickness" was unsettling. We had no other hardships. How could we complain? Things were much worse in the Northeast.

We carried on. I continued to garden and photograph nature and our neighborhood farmer. I wrote poems, too. Not about aftershocks and the radiation concern. I wrote poems about what rooted me here, about living with a Japanese family for over twenty years. The poems became my middle-grade novel *Somewhere Among*, set during the tragedies of 2001.

Eventually, I started to write *Beyond Me*. I had taken some notes, and I had my Facebook posts, emails, photos, US embassy emails, and memories as reference. I read newspapers, essays, and books; referred to earthquake data and weather reports; and rewatched and discovered footage of the disaster and its aftermath. I had to relive every aftershock. Fortunately, I was more grounded this time.

from time to time
the Earth moves

some people in the Northeast
still
live in temporary housing
the company, government, and scientists
still
tell us
radiation levels are safe
still
sunflowers won't save us yet

but
maybe someday

by observing
asking questions
taking action

with science

we will learn
how much is enough
and
someone will find
a way to clean Earth

ACKNOWLEDGMENTS

I start again with gratitude to Daddy, Carol Baker, Mrs. Eldridge, Mr. Richard Jenkins, Nancy Rinehart, and Jan Oppie, without whose early encouragement I wouldn't have continued to write and share poetry and stories.

I am grateful to my children for skyping me away from the manuscript; to Papa and friends Mari Boyle, Kathy Schmitz, Kristin Ormiston, and Cam Sato for pulling me away to do fun things; to SCBWI Japan's advisors Holly Thompson, Naomi Kojima, Mariko Nagai, and Avery Fischer Udagawa for always organizing an active calendar of events for us; to Mariko Nagai, Mari Boyle, Avery Fischer Udagawa, Emina Udagawa, and Cam Sato for reading and commenting on the story; to Mr. and Mrs. Toida for feeding our neighborhood and allowing me to photograph their work, fields, and vegetables over the years; to the Chikamatsu family for guiding me through ups and downs; to our dogs for grounding me and to our rescued cats for teaching me cat culture.

Letters and conversations about *Somewhere Among* from readers, family, and friends—especially Nancy Rinehart, The Austin Kirwans, and my mother—kept me going back to the table to finish *Beyond Me*.

Deep respect and apologies to the design team at Atheneum: Greg Stadnyk, Irene Metaxatos, and

Sonia Chaghatzbanian, for making you live through the aftershocks day after day. I am grateful for your amazing skill in making this story work visually. Thank you to Kevin Jay Stanton for creating the cover, and to Clare McGlade and Elizabeth Blake-Linn.

Deep gratitude to Caitlyn Dlouhy for her patience in letting me pursue this story at my own pace, and to Holly McGhee for making this collaboration possible.

Deepest respect and admiration for the resilience of the people of Japan, especially the people of the Northeast.